characters created by lauren child

Text based on script written by Bridget Hurst and Carol Noble

Illustrations from the TV animation produced by Tiger Aspect

With special thanks to Leigh Hodgkinson

PUFFIN BOOKS
Published by the Penguin Group: London, New York, Ireland, Australia,
Canada, India, New Zealand and South Africa
Penguin Books Ltd, Registered Offices: 80 Strand, London WC2R 0RL, England

www.penguin.com

First published 2005
This edition published 2013
001

Made and printed in China
Printed on FSC certified paper

ISBN 978-0-723-28703-2

I have this little sister Lola.
She is small and very funny.
Lola loves reading and she really loves books.
But at the moment there is
one book that is extra specially special.

One day, Lola said,
        "Charlie, Dad says he will take
us to the library and we must go
right now and get
        Beetles, Bugs and Butterflies."

Lola loves Beetles, Bugs and Butterflies.

I say,
        "But Dad took that book out
                    for you last time...
And the time before that..."

Then Lola says,
    "But Charlie, Beetles, Bugs and Butterflies is a very special book that is my favourite and I really need it.

Now.

        Now.

            Now.

                Now.

                    Now!

Don't you know
Beetles, Bugs and Butterflies
is the best book in the whole world?"

And Lola says,

"You see, Charlie,

the bugs are quite buggy

and the butterflies are really beautiful and

the beetles are...

very silly.

The beetle gets stuck! And his legs are very funny!

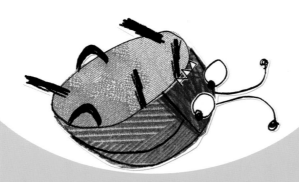

And he can't get down!"

I say,
"I know that, Lola.
Come on.
Dad's waiting."

"All his funny
little legs, Charlie!"

When we get to the library we see Lotta.
Lola says, "Lotta, I am going to get
Beetles, Bugs and Butterflies
because it is the very best book
in the world and you learn a lot
and it is very great and extremely
very interesting.
And...
And I really, really
must get it."

When we get inside
I have to say,

"Shh! Lola, it's a library.
Remember not to shout."

Lola says,
"But I can't find
my book, Charlie."

And Lotta says,
"Maybe it's over here, Lola!"

And I say, "Why don't you
try looking for it with all
the **books beginning** with **B**?"

So Lola says,
"B, B, B... Where is my book? Where can it be?"

Lotta says,
"I can't see it, Lola. It must be hiding."

I say, "You two! Stop shouting!"

Lola says, "We are not shouting, Charlie!"

I say, "Shhhhh!"

She says, "We are shushing! It's not there!
My book's not there!"

I say, "Lola! Be quiet!"
Lola says, "But Charlie, my book is lost!
It is completely not there!"

I say,
"Lola, remember this is a library
so someone must have borrowed it."

Lola says,
"But Beetles, Bugs
and Butterflies
is my book."

I say,
"But it's not your library.
Someone else obviously
wanted to read your book."

Lola says,
"But they can't. It's my book."

So I say, "Lola, just think.
There are hundreds and hundreds of other books
in the library to choose from.

There are spy books and dinosaur books. Adventure books

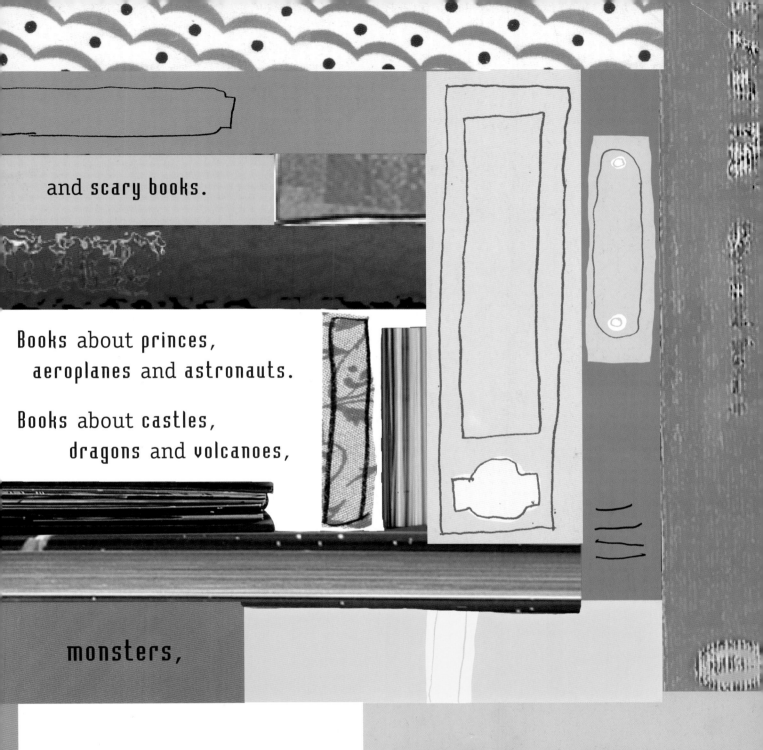

and scary books.

Books about princes,
aeroplanes and astronauts.

Books about castles,
dragons and volcanoes,

monsters,

mountains and pixies.   And books about Romans."

Romersk

فورت

România

I say,
"Look! **Romans**! This one tells you
    all about **history** in the **Roman** times.
Like how the **Romans** built long, straight roads
        and rode chariots and had
    fights with swords."

oma`11

umi

римский

ro-man

рómai

римски

로마

But Lola says,
"Too many
**big
words**,
Charlie.

Römer

zymski

Rómv

România

latinluk

So I say,
"OK, Lola, let's try to find
a book with more pictures and less words.

Lotta says, "What is this? An ency- encyclo-"
I say, "An encyclopedia! It's got millions of drawings and millions of facts.
You can learn about **everything**.
Look, this page is all about helicopters."

I say,
"You might be right, Lola,
        but see what you
   think of this...
        It's a pop-up book."

Lotta says,
   "Ooh, look at that!"

But Lola says,
   "A book that ha

cherry-blossom rain in it is **nice,** Charlie, but it's **not funny."**

Then Lola says,
"Beetles, Bugs and Butterflies
is really funny
and makes me
laugh

and

laugh

and

laugh..."

I say, "So it's an **animal** book you want.
A book with... lots of pictures... a story...
no **big** words... and animals that make you laugh."

Lola says, "Yep."

I say, "How about this one?! Cheetahs and Chimpanzees."

Lola says, "Are there
beetles, bugs and butterflies in it?!"

I say, "No, there are
cheetahs and chimpanzees.
Give it a try, Lola. Please."

Lola says, "OK, Charlie,
I will. But it won't
be as good as...

Beetles,
Bugs
and
Butterflies!
Oh no! Look!
That girl's got My book!
I don't think she knows
it is
My book!

No, noO...

Just wait...

That's **my**...

That's **my**...

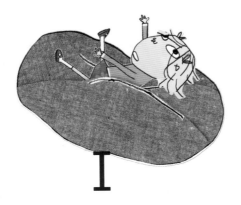

I

just

like

My book,

Charlie!"

Lola says,
"I want **my book**, Charlie!"

And I say,
"But you said you would try
          Cheetahs and Chimpanzees."

Lola says,
"Well... me and Lotta can try it, Charlie,
          but it won't be as good
     as Beetles, Bugs and Butterflies."

But then Lola says,
"Oh! Look at that. The cheetahs are very fast."
And Lotta says, "And the chimpanzees are very cheeky!"

And Lola says, "And in fact, you know what, Charlie . . . ?

This book is probably
the most best book in the whole wide world
because it is so interesting and so lovely
and you know it has the absolutely best pictures of any book ever
and the baby chimps are very funny..."